The World of Fairies

AT THE DAWN OF PIXIE HOLLOW

J
Gla

Text by Calliope Glass
Illustrated by Judith Holmes Clarke, Jeff Clark, Caroline LaVelle Egan, Denise Shimabukuro,
Adrienne Brown, Maria Elena Naggi, Charles Pickens, and the Disney Storybook Artists.
Designed by Winnie Ho

Printed in the United States of America

First Edition

10 9 8 7 6 5 4 3 2 1

ISBN 978-1-4231-0880-1

Library of Congress Cataloging-in-Publication Data on file.

Visit www.disneyfairies.com

ILS NO G942-9090-6

251 2009

SUSTAINABLE
FORESTRY
INITIATIVE

Certified Chain of Custody
40% Certified Forests,
60% Certified Fiber Sourcing

www.sfiprogram.org

PWC-SFICOC-260

For Text Pages Only

12/09
784

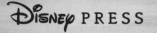

The World of Fairies

At the Dawn of Pixie Hollow

DISNEP PRESS

New York

Close your eyes and listen. Right now, half a world away, fairies are working their magic. On the enchanted isle of Never Land, they flutter from flower to tree, from brook to stream, trailing golden pixie dust as they go. If you are very, very lucky, you may hear a faint jingle or a murmuring chime carried on a chance breeze from their world to ours. You may hear them, but it is a rare thing indeed to catch a glimpse of a fairy. The Never fairies almost never leave Never Land.

But it was not always so. Once, they were as often in our world as they were in theirs. There was a time when these tiny creatures flitted from lamppost to rooftop, from country garden to forest glen, spreading their magic throughout the human world.

It was a different time, but it has not been lost from memory. Nowadays, for a fairy, or even for a lucky human, it is sometimes possible to make the journey back to that enchanted time. . . . Back to . . .

The Dawn of Pixie Hollow

The Pixie Dust Tree

Pixie Hollow, the home of the Never fairies, is a peaceful forest realm tucked away in the wilds of Never Land. At the heart of Pixie Hollow there grows a tree whose mighty trunk is a bottomless well flowing with pixie dust. The magic of the Never fairies has its source in pixie dust, so the Pixie Dust Tree is the center of all fairy life.

In fact, every fairy in Pixie Hollow discovers her life's work—her talent—in the branches of the Pixie Dust Tree.

Fairy Talents

When a fairy first arrives in Pixie Hollow, she already has a special ability; she just needs to figure out what it is. Some fairies are drawn to water, and others to plants or animals—there are even fairies who are experts on rocks, or baking cakes, or snowflakes, or fixing things. There is nothing more important to a Never fairy than her talent.

A fairy's talent is likely to affect how she dresses, where she lives, and even what she eats. But it doesn't necessarily determine her personality. Fairies who share a talent are often quite different from one another. There are water fairies who are as bubbly and impulsive as a swift brook, and others who are as calm and collected as a quiet pond.

Other Notes on Never Fairies:

- They are born of a baby's first laugh.

- They are deeply involved in the turning of the seasons and the workings of the natural world.

- They are small—roughly six inches high.

- A male fairy is sometimes called a sparrow man.

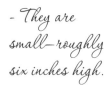

- They have a lemon-yellow glow, which can turn orange when they are embarrassed or wink out altogether when they are surprised or frightened.

Tinker Bell's Arrival

A baby's first laugh is a magical thing with a mind of its own. It rises up above the baby's crib and flies out through the nursery window. It chuckles its way over the sea, until at last it reaches Never Land. It arrives at the Pixie Dust Tree, where a sprinkling of the enchanted dust helps the laugh transform into a new fairy.

This is how nearly every fairy arrives—and Tinker Bell is no exception, although she is an exceptional fairy. When she arrived at the Pixie Dust Tree, all the other fairies hoped that she would be joining their talent group. And when her talent was revealed, the tinker fairies were overjoyed to have the new arrival take her place in their ranks. In time, Tinker Bell became Pixie Hollow's most inventive—and passionate—tinker.

THE CEREMONY

When a laugh touches down at the Pixie Dust Well and becomes a fairy, there is an ages-old ceremony that must take place. Fairies from every talent step forth to present an icon of their talent. When the newly arrived fairy passes by the icon of her talent group, it glows brightly. This is how every fairy discovers her talent.

The Tinker Talent

Tinkers' Nook

Tinkers' Nook is nestled in the roots of the Pixie Dust Tree. Many of the tinker fairies live here, in houses made of twigs and leaves. Various tunnels lead underground to the workshop, where the tinkers do much of their work. Also known as pots-and-pans fairies, tinkers are the all-purpose handy fairies of Pixie Hollow. They help fairies from other talents with repairs and mechanical problems. Their materials are twigs, acorns, pebbles, gourds, spider's silk, tree sap, Never silver, and anything else they can get their hands on.

Tinkers can mend pots, plates, shoes, wagons, pulleys, and even fairy homes. They also craft things, such as containers and shelves, and make musical instruments for the music fairies. Fairies of every talent depend on them.

Fairy Mary

Sometimes, in Pixie Hollow, a leader will emerge within a particular talent group—a fairy who excels at organization and leadership. Fairy Mary is one of these fairies. She is the undisputed head of the tinkers.

Fairy Mary and Tinker Bell are actually somewhat alike. Both fairies are passionate and headstrong, and both have short tempers. They sometimes clash, but more often Tink and Fairy Mary are united by their love of tinkering. And they are very fond of each other. Fairy Mary considers Tink to be her prodigy, and she takes great pride in Tink's achievements.

When Fairy Mary isn't tinkering or in counsel with Queen Clarion, she can often be found at the Fairy Tale Theater. She never misses a performance if she can help it.

TALENT: Tinker

LIKES: Well-oiled machines, theater

DISLIKES: Disorder

FAVORITE FOOD: Baked cranberry

FAVORITE FLOWER: Dogwood

Fairy Mary's most treasured possession is her abacus.

Tinker Bell gave Fairy Mary this pixie-dust level for her Arrival Day celebration.

A Tinker's Tools

The tinker fairies have a saying: "The difference between the right tool and almost the right tool is like the difference between a lightning bug and a pygmy glowworm with a cold." A good tinker fairy always has exactly the right tool for the job.

Shears

Chisel

Flower Sprayer

Hammer

Drill

Mortar and Pestle

Clank and Bobble Saw

Thorn Scissors

Sextant

Cheese and Blaze

Many talent groups have a few friendly animals or insects who help out with various tasks. Cheese and Blaze are the animal helpers of the tinkers. Cheese is a field mouse who spends most of his time in Tinkers' Nook. The tinkers aren't sure what his name really is, but his ears prick up when he hears the word "cheese" so that is what they call him.

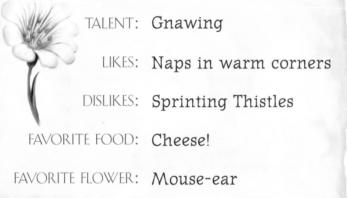

TALENT:	Gnawing
LIKES:	Naps in warm corners
DISLIKES:	Sprinting Thistles
FAVORITE FOOD:	Cheese!
FAVORITE FLOWER:	Mouse-ear

From pulling carts to gnawing through twigs, Cheese is always ready to lend a paw.

Blaze is a special friend of Tinker Bell's. She met him on an adventure, and the two quickly became inseparable. Blaze is small for a firefly but makes up for it with his big heart. He's always doing something useful, like lighting tricky corners of complicated jobs.

TALENT: Glowing

LIKES: Adventures with Tinker Bell

DISLIKES: Rats

FAVORITE FOOD: Sunflower pollen, crumbs from Tink's lunch

FAVORITE FLOWER: Azalea

Animal Friends

Though there are many working animals in Pixie Hollow, such as Cheese and Blaze, there are also creatures who are mainly just companions to the fairies. Fairies often befriend creatures related to their talents. Fast-flying fairies have a special affection for speedy birds like tree swallows. Light fairies adore fireflies, and water fairies get along very well with fish. The water fairy Silvermist even has a little goldfish in a pool at her house.

Some fairies are allergic to animals. These fairies often keep close company with spiders instead. A spider can be just as affectionate as a ladybug or a goldfinch, and it is much cuddlier than a fish (though water fairies may disagree with that).

Pixie Dust

Every Never fairy receives a sprinkling of exactly one level teacup (fairy-size, of course) of pixie dust per day. The dust is distributed at the Pixie Dust Tree by fairies of the dust-keeper talent. If a fairy can't make it to the tree, the dust talents make sure they get it to her, wherever she is.

Pixie dust aids flight, enhances magic, and acts as an all-purpose helper for fairies of every talent. Water fairies use it to get just the right sparkle on a windswept pond. Light talents make rainbows with pixie dust. And tinkers put it in nearly everything—including glue, spackle, and sandpaper. Fairies use a combination of their natural abilities and the magic of pixie dust when they are practicing their talents.

Fairies receive no more and no
less than their daily allotment
of pixie dust.

When a fairy sneezes, the
pixie dust can be temporarily
knocked off her.

The Pixie Dust Distribution Depot

The shimmering Pixie Dust Well is cupped in the heart of the Pixie Dust Tree. But fairy magic *really* shines down in the Pixie Dust Distribution Depot, at the base of the tree. Here, the dust talents sort, process, and measure out golden pixie dust. In true fairy fashion, the bustle at the depot looks chaotic, but somehow everyone always gets their daily teacupful, come rain or shine.

The Dust-Keeper Talent

Dust keepers are responsible for the collection, measurement, and distribution of pixie dust. They monitor the Pixie Dust Well and run the depot. They make sure every fairy gets one level teacup per day—no more, no less. Generally a modest talent, the dust fairies are actually some of the most important figures in Pixie Hollow.

Every dust keeper has his or her favorite teacup. Each holds exactly the same amount of dust, of course, but there is tremendous variety otherwise.

Most dust keepers don't require the daily teacup because their work keeps them thoroughly saturated with pixie dust at all times.

A Dust Keeper's Morning Route

The fairies of Pixie Hollow usually gather at the Pixie Dust Tree to receive their daily sprinkling of dust. But sometimes a fairy is too sick or too busy to come by. It's especially common for fairies to be too busy to come get their daily dust during the turning of a season, when every fairy in Pixie Hollow—and on the mainland—is working as hard as she can.

That's when dust keepers like Terence step in and start delivering pixie dust personally. Terence is a sociable fellow, so he always enjoys visiting fairies in their homes or workshops to deliver a sprinkling of dust and have a conversation. And if Tinker Bell is one of the fairies on his list, so much the better. Terence and Tink are the best of friends, and Terence is always happy for the chance to say hello and admire whatever new invention Tink is working on.

Here is a map showing Terence's delivery rounds on a typical busy morning in Pixie Hollow.

Pixie Dustology and the Hall of Scepters

Some dust keepers are great scholars. Since pixie dust is the most important element of the Never fairies' magic, they have always been eager to understand it as well as they can. There are even fairies who devote their whole lives to studying its properties and recording the results of their experiments. This field is called pixie dustology, and there is an entire section of the library filled with tomes of its lore. Pixie dustologists can often be found among these stacks of books, or in a little room in the Pixie Dust Tree where they keep their extensive collection of dust samples. Countless little jars each contain a bit of pixie dust from every season as far back as fairy memory goes.

Blue Pixie Dust

Once in a great while, a blue moon rises over Pixie Hollow.

This is a signal to the fairies that the time has come for the Pixie Dust Tree to be rejuvenated. A fairy is chosen to craft a scepter, and when the light of the blue moon shines through the moonstone in the scepter, it creates *blue pixie dust*. This dust has the power to replenish the tree. If the Pixie Dust Tree is not replenished every blue moon, it will wither, and the pixie dust will flow no more.

Once, it was Tinker Bell's job to create a new scepter to hold the moonstone. Her efforts took her far and wide, all across Never Land, and beyond its shores. In fact, she almost wasn't ready when the blue moon reached its peak. But Tink prevailed, and the tree was saved again. And now Tinker Bell's scepter has joined countless other masterworks in a chamber of the Pixie Dust Tree known as the Hall of Scepters.

Fairy Gary

Just as Fairy Mary has become the undisputed leader of the tinker talent,
Fairy Gary is in charge of the dust-keeper fairies. Most often to be found at
the Pixie Dust Distribution Depot, Fairy Gary has a genius for organization.
All the other dust talents report to him throughout the day on the level of
the Well, on any variations in the quality of dust it produces, and on whether
any fairies have missed their daily teacup. Based on this information, Fairy
Gary makes the decisions that keep the dust flowing freely and the depot
running smoothly.

TALENT: Dust keeper

LIKES: Making improvements to the depot

DISLIKES: Having to fish lost objects out of the Pixie Dust Well

FAVORITE FOOD: Acorn stews

FAVORITE FLOWER: Orchid

There are fourteen different fairy languages and dialects in the world, and Fairy Gary knows how to say "pixie dust" in every one of them.

PIXIE-DUST DIVING

Occasionally a fairy will accidentally drop something in the Pixie Dust Well. (Usually a shoe or a button, but on one memorable occasion, an entire mouse-drawn wagon.) When this happens, Fairy Gary dons his diving suit and goes "fishing."

Pixie Dust in Fairy Home Life

Hoarding Pixie Dust

Just because a fairy receives a teacupful of dust every day doesn't mean she *uses* a teacupful every day. Many fairies set aside a little bit from their daily sprinkle for special projects.

Iridessa, for example, has been filling a glass lantern bit by bit with pixie dust. When it is full she plans on giving it to her friend Fira, another light talent, to hang in her room.

One garden talent keeps her extra dust all to herself!

Some fairies have pet plants that get a little pixie dust with their daily watering.

Pixie-Dust Tools

Fairy Gary doesn't need to hoard pixie dust—he's permanently dusty from his job and has plenty to spare. But he does have a collection of a different kind.

The largest teacup collection in Pixie Hollow, and probably in all of Never Land, can be found in Fairy Gary's home. His teacups are of all shapes, but each holds exactly one level teacupful—just the right amount for a fairy's daily sprinkle.

It has taken Fairy Gary many years to build his collection. He found some of the cups, but most of them were gifts. When Fairy Gary's Arrival Day rolls around, his friends always know what to give him.

Fairy Gary is especially proud of one teacup in his collection. Tinker Bell found it washed up on the shore of Never Land. It was part of a human toy fairy tea-set, and it is precisely the same size as a real fairy teacup!

The Mainland

Fairies and Nature

The Never fairies spend much of their time working to bring the seasons to the human world, which they call the mainland. These tiny creatures are responsible for many of the most treasured aspects of each season—painting flowers in springtime, ripening plums in summer, creating brisk autumn breezes, and carving snowflakes in winter.

The preparation for a coming season can take months. While some fairies are busy with winter on the mainland, others back in Pixie Hollow are already gathering supplies for spring. There are rainbows to be made, spring showers to be bottled, ladybugs to be painted, and seeds to be sorted and packed.

When it is time for the turning of the seasons on the mainland, the fairies assemble all their supplies, which are packed into baskets and boxes and bags, and fly to the mainland in a grand procession across the sea. Once they arrive, they begin the happy work of ushering in the season.

Every fairy has a part to play in the turning of the seasons, even sour-tempered Vidia. This fast-flying fairy creates wind to funnel pollen out of flowers during the preparations for spring.

The Queen

The turning of the seasons is overseen by the fairies' queen, Clarion. No one in Pixie Hollow knows if Queen Clarion ever had a traditional talent like the other fairies do. For as far back as anyone can remember, she has led and inspired all the fairy talents.

Clarion is certainly the most powerful fairy in Pixie Hollow. Her understanding of fairy magic is so complete that she often travels as a beam of pure pixie dust. She may sometimes seem remote, but there has never been a kinder queen. Although she can be firm when it is called for, Clarion is evenhanded and understanding. She loves all her fairy subjects, and she would do anything for them.

Queen Clarion is set apart from the other fairies by her large wings, her pixie-dust–hemmed gown, and, of course, her sparkling tiara.

Fairy Jewelry

Fairies, like birds, are attracted to anything that glitters and shines—especially jewels and precious metals. You would be hard-pressed to find a fairy who doesn't have a few treasured pieces in her jewelry box. Fairy jewelry tends to be highly detailed and dazzlingly shiny. Some pieces are made by the fairies themselves, and others are found objects or gifts from other creatures.

Tinker Bell has a bracelet that she made herself, from a Never silver fairy fork. She only wears it on special occasions, because she doesn't want it to get dented or scratched. The light fairy Iridessa likes to wear glittering clips of polished mica in her hair every now and then. And even no-frills Fawn has a seed bracelet made for her by a friendly shrew.

Fairies and Humans

When the fairies of Pixie Hollow travel to the mainland, they try to avoid being seen by humans. They do much of their work at night. In the daytime, fairy scouts stationed high in the trees keep a close eye out for humans.

Despite their care, fairies are sometimes spotted. Occasionally, a human child will catch a glimpse of a shining wing or see the glow of a fairy moving through a garden late at night. And, although they prefer to work unseen, fairies like to make their presence felt in other ways. If a human child leaves an offering of honey and milk in an acorn cap, a fairy will be happy to help herself. She may even leave a little present as a thank-you.

The Scout Talent

The scouts have plenty to do in Pixie Hollow, where they keep fairies safe from dangers, such as hawks, storms, and wasps. But they have a lot of work on the mainland as well. These dedicated, hyperalert pixies perch on strategic posts and keep watch for nosy humans. When a human is spotted, the scouts sound a warning, and all the fairies know to make themselves scarce.

The scout talents have a number of tools of the trade. Every scout carries a set of twig-and-leaf binoculars, an ultra–high-frequency whistle (so high only a fairy can hear it), and a bow and arrow.

Kensington Gardens

Although the fairies of Never Land bring the seasons to every nook and corner of the mainland, there are some spots they especially like to visit. One of these spots is Kensington Gardens, a beautiful park in London, England. It is a lush oasis of nature in the middle of the city.

The fairies' attraction to Kensington Gardens has led to more than the usual number of sightings by humans. As a result, the fairies have become associated with Kensington Gardens in human folklore.

Never Land

The Inhabitants of Never Land

As fond as the fairies are of the mainland, their true home is Never Land. This magical island is not on any map. Indeed, it floats freely across the sea and goes wherever it likes. If Never Land does not want to be found, it won't be. But if it welcomes you, you will have no trouble making your way to it.

In addition to the fairies, Never Land is also home to a few humans. Captain Hook and his pirates spend most of their time in their ship, the *Jolly Roger*—anchored in the cove or sailing in the waters off the coast of Never Land. And Peter Pan and his Lost Boys live in a hideout in the densest part of Never Land's jungle.

Visit Mermaid Lagoon, and you may catch a glimpse of a mermaid sunning herself on a rock. A climb up Torth Mountain will bring you to the cave where the dragon Kyto is imprisoned. And if you make the perilous trek north of Never Land, you may even meet a pair of trolls.

Peter Pan's drawing of Never Land may be crude,
but it's the most complete map anyone knows of.

The Trolls

Tinker Bell is one of the few fairies who have journeyed over the sea, far north of Never Land. She went there in search of the mythical Mirror of Incanta, which was held by fairy lore to be in a pirate shipwreck. She found the mirror, but she also made some other astonishing discoveries on her journey, including the bridge trolls.

These two creatures guard a bridge on Lost Island, north of Never Land. Though they do their best to scare off any passing travelers, they often get distracted while squabbling with each other. Anyone wishing to cross the bridge must simply get them into an argument and slip past.

TALENT: Bridge-guarding (though they aren't very good at it)

LIKES: Frightening travelers; insulting each other

DISLIKES: Being outsmarted

FAVORITE FOOD: Fairy bones, they claim . . . but nobody's ever seen them eat *anything*.

FAVORITE FLOWER: They prefer mushrooms.

The shorter troll has a pet rock named Harold.

Fairy Modes of Travel

Tinker Bell was able to travel off to the northern tip of Never Land, but she couldn't do it by herself. A fairy has only a day's worth of fairy dust on her, and without the enchanted dust, fairy wings can only keep their owners in the air for a few moments at a time. The fairies call this dustless fluttering "chicken flying."

When Tinker Bell traveled north, she invented a balloon carrier so she wouldn't have to walk once her dust ran out. Since then, these carriers have become a routine way of getting from point A to point B for the Never fairies. But the fairies have many other clever modes of transportation besides balloon carriers.

Fairies also travel by boat (usually made of leaves or bark), raft (bark or twigs), cart (twigs again), and, of course, on the backs of their animal friends. Some fairies use their talents to create vehicles: light fairies run across rainbows, and water fairies create waves to surf on.

If you're not in a hurry,
traveling "on the snail
shell" is a very dependable
way of getting somewhere.
But keep in mind it may
take you several weeks.

65

Fairy Helpers

On any given day in Pixie Hollow, the Never fairies have many important tasks to accomplish. Luckily, much of their work is aided by their animal and insect friends. The scout fairies, with the help of animal talents, train bugs, mice, and even small predators to keep Pixie Hollow safe. Birds, butterflies, and bats assist in moving supplies from Never Land to the mainland during the changing of the seasons. Messenger pigeons carry notes across Pixie Hollow. Friendly spiders weave fabric, which is used for clothing, decorations, nets, and ropes.

Every once in a while the fairies will find a baby animal that has been orphaned or lost. On one memorable occasion, the animal fairies found an orphaned wildcat kitten. This kitten was taken in by the scout fairies who, with help from the animal talents, trained it to go on patrol. Pixie Hollow has never had a fiercer protector than that wildcat, who was named Tiny by the scouts.

Fawn

The animal fairy Fawn is bold, brave, and a bit of a rascal. This merry fairy is always ready to play, and the more rough-and-tumble the game, the better. Fawn is mischievous and a born prankster—she likes to play tricks on her friend Iridessa. She speaks many different animal languages, but the burplike toad-speak is her favorite.

Like a mockingbird, Fawn can replicate any birdsong if she hears it just once. She uses this talent frequently, talking easily with any bird. The other animal talents know to go to Fawn if they want to hear the latest Pixie Hollow avian gossip.

Fawn isn't all pranks and tale-telling, though. She's got a heart the size of a watermelon, and it shows. There's nobody as patient and kind when teaching baby birds to fly in the spring or when singing bears to sleep in the winter.

TALENT: Animal

LIKES: Leapfrog, fairy tag

DISLIKES: Wing-washing time

FAVORITE FOOD: Melted acorn butter, on anything

FAVORITE FLOWER: Tiger lily

Fawn's favorite toy is a hedgehog made from a horse chestnut. This was a gift from Tinker Bell for Fawn's Arrival Day. She keeps it safe at home so as to avoid having one of her animal friends eat it by accident.

Pixie Hollow

A Fairy Paradise

Pixie Hollow is truly a hidden haven in the wilds of Never Land. Surrounded by hills and mountains, the fairies' home is a wide forest valley spotted with streams, flower patches, and meadows. All the Never fairies live here, along with many of their animal friends.

The magnificent Pixie Dust Tree grows in the very center of Pixie Hollow. Its roots extend all the way to the edges of the realm, and the tree spreads its magic throughout this enchanted valley. Queen Clarion and the Ministers of the Seasons live high in its branches, but the rest of the fairies have their homes tucked away here and there throughout the valley.

Pixie Hollow is divided into four areas, one for each season. These seasonal realms do not change—it is always winter in Winter Woods, for instance. Springtime Square, Summer Glade, and Autumn Forest are also each eternally in the height of their respective seasons, and in a miracle of fairy magic, these neighborhoods sit side-by-side throughout the year.

Life in Pixie Hollow is busy, because fairies enjoy the hustle and bustle of their work. But these tiny creatures never forget to take a break to enjoy the beauty of the world around them.

Fairy Leadership

Queen Clarion rules over Pixie Hollow, but no one fairy—not even the queen—can keep track of all the details involved in bringing the seasons to the mainland. Luckily, Pixie Hollow has four ministers. These fairies each organize and direct a different season, and they all report to Queen Clarion.

THE COUNCIL CHAMBERS

The council chambers are in the Pixie Dust Tree, not far from the rooms where Queen Clarion and the ministers live. There, the queen meets with her ministers and other important figures, such as Fairy Mary and Fairy Gary.

Culture in Pixie Hollow

Fairy life is filled with many different forms of art and creative expression. Some fairies are born to it—the painting talents, or the reed-flute players, or the wind dancers. But even those fairies whose talents lie in other directions have their moments of artistic inspiration. A water fairy, for example, can never help bursting into song on a rainy day.

Art is also one of the ways fairies preserve their history. A stained-glass window in the Pixie Dust Tree tells the story of Winda Quickwing, a legendary hero of Pixie Hollow. And of course, there's Fairy Tale Theater, where depictions of fairy myths and histories are spun out of pixie dust itself.

THE FAIRY DANCE

The Fairy Dance brings together the arts of dance, music, and fashion at every full moon. Even the ever-busy light fairy Fira takes time to put on a new dress and enjoy herself at the dance.

Fairy Tale Theater

Nestled under a mossy awning at the base of the Pixie Dust Tree, Fairy Tale Theater is a large space, complete with stage and orchestra, where the storytelling fairies spin their tales. These shows are elaborate creations—music, lights, and special effects from pixie dust combine to make an otherworldly experience for the audience.

Some of the stories told in Fairy Tale Theater are based on popular fairy folklore. Some are reenactments of fairy history. And some are plain old fiction. Whatever the content, the fairies of Pixie Hollow love to gather together in the mossy amphitheater and watch the storytellers work their magic. Fairy Mary is an especially big fan—she never misses a play.

The Storytelling Talent

Storytellers are the keepers of fairy legends and tales. If a story's ever been told in Pixie Hollow, there's sure to be a storyteller who knows it. As a result, these fairies are the unofficial historians of Never Land. A storyteller is likely to know anything that can be found in the library—and many things that can't be.

In public performances, the storytellers use verse and other poetic language to tell their stories. They create pixie-dust animations to bring the stories to life. This tends to be especially effective when a scary story is being told.

Most of the time, the storytellers do their work at Fairy Tale Theater. But occasionally they can be persuaded to tell a little anecdote—or even a joke—in a quieter setting.

Storytellers tend to be wise about fairy nature and can give useful advice.

Lyria

Lyria is one of the greatest storytellers the talent has ever known. Her specialty is spinning grand, epic tales based on fairy legend. Lyria has brought the art of pixie-dust illustration to a new level, often creating startlingly lifelike accompaniments to her stories. Her performances can last for hours, but her audience is always so wrapped up in the story they hardly notice the time.

Despite her confidence on the stage, Lyria can be quite shy in person. Only her closest friends know her greatest wish: to travel to the mainland and see a human play.

TALENT:	Storyteller
LIKES:	Being onstage
DISLIKES:	Losing her voice
FAVORITE FOOD:	Carrot soup
FAVORITE FLOWER:	Trumpet flower

Lyria drinks lemongrass tea with agave nectar to soothe her throat after telling a long story.

Seasonal Talents

Most fairies have talents that serve all four seasons, whether directly or indirectly. The storytellers, for instance, inspire all the fairies to do the best work they can. The garden talents lend their green thumbs mainly to spring and summer, but there's always work for them in autumn and winter as well. Every season has need of the water fairies, the tinkers, even the fast-flying fairies.

But there are some fairies who specialize in only one season. These fairies have a talent that is uniquely suited for a particular time of the year. Some examples include snowflake fairies (winter), pumpkin-plumping garden fairies (autumn), summer rain fairies (summer), and leaf-unfurling fairies (spring).

When these fairies are not stationed on the mainland overseeing their season, they are camped out in one of the four seasonal areas of Pixie Hollow, honing their crafts.

Spring Valley

The Minister of Spring

Although spring is a wild, merry, and carefree season, the Minster of Spring is not any of those things. The minister imposes perfect order on the preparations for his season. It's a good thing, too—things have a way of getting out of hand, what with garden fairies chasing baby flower bulbs about and animal fairies teaching fledglings to fly.

As serious as he is, the Minister of Spring is known for his kindness, especially to plants. Some garden fairies speculate that he was a garden talent before becoming the minister, but nobody knows for sure.

TALENT:	Minister
LIKES:	Orderly rows of springtime supplies
DISLIKES:	Unexpected problems (somehow Tinker Bell is always involved)
FAVORITE FOOD:	Fiddlehead fern
FAVORITE FLOWER:	Camellias (the first to bloom in the spring)

The Minister of Spring usually wears a neatly cut suit of spring blooms.

The Minister of Spring has a pet crocus that sits in a pot on his windowsill.

Tinker Bell's Inventions

The Minister of Spring is already a little high-strung, but he always looks even more nervous than usual when Tinker Bell is around. There is a reason for this.

When Tinker Bell first arrived in Never Land, the preparations for spring were well underway. But Tink, who was newly arrived and inexperienced, made a few mistakes—and they weren't small ones. Disaster ensued, and spring nearly had to be canceled. Luckily, this calamity caused Tink to find her true vocation: inventing. She whipped up a number of time-saving devices, and the fairies were able to put spring back together just in time to bring it to the mainland.

Since then, Tink's inventions have made all the seasons happen more smoothly and efficiently. And all the ministers are grateful to her for her help.

Tink's inventions can
be found all across
Pixie Hollow.

Painting the Seasons

Tinker Bell's paintball thrower certainly makes the springtime
ladybug-painting go faster. But it isn't the most accurate tool.
When a keen eye for color is needed, expert painters step in.

Iridessa

One of the most talented light fairies, Iridessa is a perfectionist. She's passionate about her work, but she's easily stressed—although she tries to look on the bright side of things, she often spies disaster lurking. But she's right more often than she's wrong, so the other fairies usually listen to her.

Iridessa is a bit of a know-it-all, but that's one of the things her friends love about her. What other fairy knows the name of every single firefly in Pixie Hollow? Who else has identified thirty-four distinct ways to fold a sunbeam? Iridessa is one of a kind.

TALENT: Light

LIKES: Knowing the right answer

DISLIKES: Not knowing the right answer

FAVORITE FOOD: Lemon-meringue pie

FAVORITE FLOWER: Sunflower

Iridessa invented a popular fairy drink: lemonade with bubbles of sunlight in it. Be warned—a case of the hiccups after a glass of "Dess-ade" can be almost blinding!

Fireflies in Pixie Hollow

Each day at twilight, Iridessa and her friends gather the last sunbeams of the evening and use them to help light the fireflies. This ensures that the work of bringing the seasons to the mainland can continue well into the dark of the night.

Fireflies are very useful to the fairies, whose glows are not always bright enough to light their way.

Fairy Games

The fireflies aren't the only creatures in Pixie Hollow who like to play. Many of the fairies' games involve their other animal and insect friends. For example: pill-bug marbles, where the pill bugs steer themselves as they roll.

Another favorite is the hummingbird reverse race. Here, the fairy whose hummingbird gets to the finish line last, wins. (Hummingbirds are very impatient, so it's hard to keep them from trying to get there first.)

Some fairy games are just for fairies. Three-winged races are a great favorite in Summer Glade.

Summer Glade

The Minister of Summer

It's quite possible that no one in Pixie Hollow enjoys her job quite as much as the Minister of Summer. In fact, it may be the case that no one enjoys *anything* as much as this free-spirited fairy. She has a merry, ringing laugh—when something funny happens in Summer Glade, they can hear her laughing all the way over in Winter Woods.

Unlike the Minister of Spring, the Minister of Summer is not terribly interested in organization. But she's unflappable and hardworking, and her summers on the mainland are always a success.

The Minister of Summer is always dressed in summer blossoms.

TALENT: Minister

LIKES: Currant punch and summer breezes

DISLIKES: Spoilsports and fussbudgets

FAVORITE FOOD: Wild strawberries

FAVORITE FLOWER: Hollyhock

The Minister of Summer has nearly twenty combs, but none of them is up to the task of taming her curly mane. The coiffure-talent fairies keep trying, though. Every year on her Arrival Day they give her another one.

Fairy Gifts

Fairies love to give each other presents. They have plenty of opportunities: in Pixie Hollow, gifts are usually exchanged on Arrival Days, during the turning of the seasons, at the Fairy Dance, at tea parties, or just because.

Fairy gifts are often handmade. A fairy may also give an interesting found object if it reminds her of her friend. And even though fairies especially like leaving surprise presents for each other, you can often tell the talent of the gift giver by the way the present is wrapped. For example, if a gift is wrapped in spider lace, it may be from an animal fairy. If it is wrapped in blueprint paper, you can bet it's from a tinker fairy.

If it is wrapped in flower petals, it is probably from a garden fairy.

Wrapped in a bubble? Water fairy.

Fairies and Water

Fairies—all fairies, not just the water talents—love water.

Silvermist

Water fairy Silvermist (Sil, to her friends) has a wonderfully offbeat way of looking at the world. Free-spirited and optimistic, she sometimes listens to her heart more than her head, and that can get her into trouble every now and then. But she's easygoing and affectionate, and impossible not to love. And although she and Iridessa could not be less alike, the two fairies are very close.

There's a saying in Pixie Hollow: "Water fairies have more fun." In Silvermist's case, it may just be true. Whether stopping by the babbling brook to catch up on Pixie Hollow gossip, telling jokes to her pet goldfish, or learning to juggle raindrops, Silvermist enjoys life to the fullest.

TALENT: Water

LIKES: When everyone gets along

DISLIKES: Loud noises

FAVORITE FOOD: Water chestnuts

FAVORITE FLOWER: Water lily

Silvermist's prized possession is a perfume mister . . . filled with water. What more welcome fragrance is there for a water fairy?

Fairy Fashions

Silvermist, like many water fairies, can make gorgeous, though short-lived,
garments and jewels out of water. Her friends especially love to wear these
cool, beautiful creations on a hot summer's day.

Other fairies are just as inventive
when it comes to fashion. Here, a
human's handkerchief becomes a
simple sundress for a fairy.

Lost Things

"Lost things" are what fairies call the trinkets from the mainland that wash up on the shores of Never Land. They find coins, jewelry, gears, bolts, even toys. Before Tinker Bell arrived, these things were thought to be useless to fairies. But Tink found a use for them by creating tools to save spring.

Tinker Bell pioneered the idea of using lost things in inventions, and there are now many uses for human objects in Pixie Hollow.

Silvermist uses a silver spoon to waterski.

Tink's bed is made
from a seashell.

Rosetta has yet to figure out what
her beautiful new vase used to be.

Autumn Forest

The Minister of Autumn

Wise and logical, the Minister of Autumn is hard to fluster. He oversees the preparations for autumn with a steady hand and a kind word for every fairy. Generally hands-off, the Minister of Autumn would rather trust the fairies in his charge to do their jobs well than get in their way. But when the time comes to bring autumn to the mainland, he can be found in the thick of things, ensuring that nothing goes wrong.

The Minister of Autumn makes his home in Autumn Forest. His house doesn't have glass in the windows—he likes to feel the crisp fall breeze all the time.

TALENT: Minister

LIKES: A perfectly plump pumpkin

DISLIKES: Early frosts

FAVORITE FOOD: Butternut squash

FAVORITE FLOWER: Goldenrod

The Minister of Autumn usually wears a suit of orange, brown, and red leaves.

His preferred method of transportation is riding on the fallen leaf of a sycamore tree and being whisked along by the wind.

Obscure Talents

The turning of any season requires the work of all sorts of fairies. But it takes some of the most specialized talents to bring autumn.

Take, for example, the early-frost-warning talents: they sit quietly on the mainland during the fall, and watch for an unseasonable chill. And then there are the crisp-fall-breeze specialists from the fast-flying talent. And don't forget about the pumpkin-plumping fairies.

The hibernation bedtime-story fairies are a subset of the animal talent, though the storyteller talents often try to claim them as their own.

Fairy Foods

Fairies are great gardeners, and they love to eat fresh fruits and vegetables. Some of the best food in Pixie Hollow is harvested in Autumn Forest, where there is a splendid pumpkin patch and an apple tree with the sweetest, juiciest apples. These plants are looked after by the garden fairies, who can always tell when a vine wants something to lean on, when a tree needs a little extra room, or when a squash is perfectly ripe.

Crab-Apple Jelly

1 crab apple
140 acorn caps
beet sugar

Select one firm crab apple. Wash and remove blossom ends. Dice and place in large pot. Add water to cover crab-apple pieces and boil until fruit is soft.

Strain the crab-apple juice through spiderweb-jelly cloth. Heat crab-apple juice and add sugar. Boil, stirring constantly, until it thickens.

Ladle into acorn caps to cool. Sprinkle with sugar and serve.

Caution—may still be too sour for some fairies. Add more sugar to taste.

Fairies hate to let anything go to waste, so they even eat the fruit of sour plum trees, although they have to be a bit inventive about it.

Wheat kernels are just the right size for a fairy snack on the go.

Rosetta

Rosetta is a garden fairy. She has excellent manners, but she's also very quick-witted. Rosetta always tries to look her best, and she loves giving beauty tips to her friends—and her flowers!

Fairies don't age, of course, but Rosetta arrived in Pixie Hollow before most of her friends—so she's a little wiser than they are. She's also had more time to collect shoes. In fact, Rosetta has more pairs of shoes than any other fairy in the history of Pixie Hollow. And because she almost always flies to get where she's going, most of her shoes are entirely decorative.

Rosetta is the inventor of the flower parasol.

TALENT: Gardening

LIKES: Flower painting

DISLIKES: Poor hygiene

FAVORITE FOOD: Buttercup soup

FAVORITE FLOWER: Wild rose

THE ARRIVAL GOWN

Although she has many beautiful
and elaborate dresses, Rosetta's
favorite is the gown she arrived
in. She keeps it on a special
hanger in a special wardrobe
and never wears it.

Fairy Homes

There are tiny fairy homes tucked here
and there throughout every corner of Pixie
Hollow. Fairies work hard to decorate
their homes to suit their personalities.
Rosetta's home—made of flowers, with a
chimney from a human's watering can—
suits her just fine.

Iridessa's home is another beauty. It's admired by other light fairies for its spectacular cut-glass-bowl dome and the huge quartz crystal set at the peak. And the tinker fairies are impressed by its innovative use of a human object (Tink helped out, but it was Iridessa's idea). The prisms formed by the many facets of the cut-glass roof give Iridessa plenty of rainbows to look at when she's at home.

Winter Woods

The Minister of Winter

The Minister of Winter is a blunt, uncompromising fairy. She knows how to get the job done, and she isn't interested in nonsense. What nobody in Pixie Hollow knows is that the Minister of Winter does have one impractical secret habit: she washes her hair in ice water to make it shiny. It's a tip she acquired from Rosetta, who has vowed to keep quiet.

The Minister of Winter is too busy to be vain, however. In addition to leading the annual effort to bring winter to the mainland, the Minister has identified seventeen different classes of snowflake. She is considered a great scholar of snow.

TALENT: Minister

LIKES: Efficiency

DISLIKES: Distractions

FAVORITE FOOD: Roasted chestnuts

FAVORITE FLOWER: January jasmine

The Minister of Winter wears a gown woven from fine threads of frost.

Fairies and Snow

Winter Fairies love to play in the snow! Whether skating down a frozen stream or building tiny snow forts, there's always plenty of fun for fairies to have in Winter Woods.

Fairy Winter Wear

Outside of snowflake and frost talents, Never fairies can't take the cold of Winter Woods for very long. So if they are going to play in the snow, they need to bundle up much more than usual!

Fairies wear all sorts of hats, but Fawn's favorite is an old hummingbird nest.

Triple-ply spider silk is an elegant solution for cold weather—it's very warm but not at all bulky or awkward.

Some fairies prefer to use pygmy-goose down for stuffing their jackets.

Dandelion fluff is an excellent liner for capes and boots.

Fairy Holidays and Celebrations

As busy as the Never fairies are bringing the seasons to the mainland, they always find time to relax and enjoy themselves. A fairy's Arrival Day—the yearly anniversary of the day she came into being in Pixie Hollow—is always celebrated by her friends.

And then there are celebrations for each season, such as the autumn revelry, which marks the end of fall, and the blooming of the everblossom, which marks the beginning of spring. And sometimes, there is no reason. After all, if a fairy feels like having a midnight tea party with her best friend, who is to stop her?

Clank and Bobble

Clank and Bobble are both tinkers. They're good-natured fellows and best friends, and they were the first fairies to befriend Tinker Bell when she arrived in Never Land.

Clank is a big, boisterous sparrow man who sometimes plugs his ears with fluff when he's hammering things. Bobble is short compared to other fairies, and he wears dewdrop goggles for detail work.

Clank and Bobble both wear leaf overalls made from the toughest fronds they could find.

TALENT: Tinkers

LIKES: Finding just the right twig for an axle

DISLIKES: Getting in trouble with Fairy Mary

FAVORITE FOOD: Mashed potatoes (Clank), mashed turnips (Bobble)

FAVORITE FLOWER: Pinecone (Bobble—"Technically, it is a flower!"), hibiscus (Clank—"It's the biggest one there is!")

Once, for a practical joke, Clank replaced the dewdrops in Bobble's eye-dropper with rosewater, and Bobble spent a good hour convinced Pixie Hollow had turned pink overnight!

Fairy Friendships

Fairies are affectionate creatures. They tend to develop long-lasting friendships—usually with other fairies. But occasionally an especially shy animal fairy will become best friends with, say, a field mouse—and there's at least one garden fairy who has made a geranium her closest confidante.

Geraniums are excellent secret-keepers.

Everyday Magic

Somewhere, the island of Never Land is bobbing in the sea. On that enchanted isle, some of the fairies of Pixie Hollow are talking, laughing, and singing. Others are sitting quietly, enjoying the beauty and magic of their world.

And although an ordinary human will hardly ever set foot in their world . . .

. . . the fairies will always bring
a little bit of magic to ours.